A NOTE ABOUT THE STORY

Like the talented storyteller who shares her version with us now, this enchanting cumulative tale has roots in many Spanish-speaking countries around the world, where it has found a delighted audience of children. Alma Flor Ada's first memories of the tale are of hearing it as a little girl in Cuba from her grandmother, who would vary the story's form to fit their surroundings. If they were on the porch, for instance, and a rider on horseback came down the road, it would be a horse who refused to eat the grass. If they were lying on her grandmother's hammock by the river and a cow was grazing nearby, it would be a cow in the story. Today, the author tells us, "I have rejoiced seeing the bright, attentive eyes of children waiting in suspense as I try to render the increasingly long list of animals in one breath!"

The art for the story blends the tropical hues of Cuba with costume and architectural references to other Spanish-speaking countries, in acknowledgment of the story's presence in so many different cultures. Kathleen Kuchera created each picture by first cutting a zinc plate to size. She then engraved the image on the metal using a dry point needle, and made a print from the engraved plate. To these prints the artist added the brilliant colors that are true both to Kathleen Kuchera's personality and to the charming, sunny story itself.

—*Tomie dePaola, Creative Director*
WHITEBIRD BOOKS

For Alfonso, this most favorite tale of his childhood. —A. F. A.

To my family, with love. —K. K.

G. P. Putnam's Sons, a division of The Putnam & Grosset Group,
200 Madison Avenue, New York, NY 10016. Published simultaneously in Canada.
Printed in Hong Kong by South China Printing Co. (1988) Ltd.
Book design by Gunta Alexander. The text is set in Worcester Round
Library of Congress Cataloging-in-Publication Data
Ada, Alma Flor.   The rooster who went to his uncle's wedding :
a Latin American folktale / retold by Alma Flor Ada ; illustrated by Kathleen Kuchera.
p.   cm.   "A Whitebird book." Summary: In this cumulative folktale from
Latin America, the sun sets off a chain of events which results in the cleaning
of Rooster's beak in time for his uncle's wedding.
[1. Folklore—Latin America.]   I. Kuchera, Kathleen. ill.   II. Title.   PZ8.1.A218
1993   398.2—dc20   [E]   92-14087   CIP   AC
ISBN 0-399-22412-2
1 3 5 7 9 10 8 6 4 2
First Impression

The Rooster
Who Went to His Uncle's Wedding

A LATIN AMERICAN FOLKTALE
RETOLD BY ALMA FLOR ADA
ILLUSTRATED BY KATHLEEN KUCHERA

A WHITEBIRD BOOK
G. P. Putnam's Sons
New York

Early one morning, when the sun had not yet appeared, the rooster of this story was busy shining his beak and combing up his feathers. It was the day of his uncle's wedding, and the rooster wanted to be on time.

When everything looked perfect he set off down the road with a brisk and springy walk. With each step the rooster nodded his head, thinking of all the wonderful things waiting for him at the wedding banquet.

Before long his stomach began to growl. "I wish I'd eaten breakfast," he said. Then something caught his eye. There, next to the road, sat a single golden kernel of corn.

Perfect, the rooster thought. But when he got closer he could see that the kernel was lying in a puddle of mud. If he ate it he would get his beak all dirty.

Oh, that rooster was hungry. But he couldn't go to his uncle's wedding with a dirty beak. *What to do? Peck or not peck?* he wondered.

The rooster stared at the kernel.

Then with one sharp peck he gobbled it down...and wound up with a beak full of mud.

So the rooster looked around quickly for someone who could help him. First he noticed the grass growing on the side of the road.

The rooster said to the grass:

"Dear grass, velvety grass,

won't you please clean my beak

so that I can go to my own uncle's wedding?"

But the grass answered:

"No, I won't. Why should I?"

The rooster looked around to see if there was anyone else who could help him. Just then he saw a lamb grazing in the field. Maybe he could *scare* the grass into helping. So he asked the lamb:

"Dear lamb, woolly lamb,

please eat the grass

that won't clean my beak

so that I can go to my own uncle's wedding."

But the lamb answered:

"No, I won't. Why should I?"

The rooster strutted back and forth in dismay. But then he saw a dog walking on the road. So he asked the dog:

"Dear dog, fierce dog,

please bite the lamb

that won't eat the grass

that won't clean my beak

so that I can go to my own uncle's wedding."

But the dog answered:

"No, I won't. Why should I?"

Well, this rooster was not one to give up. So he went over to a stick lying by the road. And he asked it:

"Dear stick, hard stick,

please hit the dog

that won't bite the lamb

that won't eat the grass

that won't clean my beak

so that I can go to my own uncle's wedding."

But the stick answered:

"No, I won't. Why should I?"

The rooster was starting to worry. But he looked around for someone else to help, and he spotted a campfire the shepherds had lit. He got close to the fire and asked:

"Dear fire, bright fire,
please burn the stick
that won't hit the dog
that won't bite the lamb
that won't eat the grass
that won't clean my beak
so that I can go to my own uncle's wedding."
But the fire answered:
"No, I won't. Why should I?"

The rooster ruffled his feathers and paced. Would anyone be able to help him in time? Then he noticed a brook crossing the field. He bent over and whispered, as sincerely as he could:

"Dear water, clear water,

please put out the fire

that won't burn the stick

that won't hit the dog

that won't bite the lamb

that won't eat the grass

that won't clean my beak

so that I can go to my own uncle's wedding."

But the water answered:

"No, I won't. Why should I?"

Now the poor rooster couldn't think of anyone else to ask for help. He lifted his muddy beak up and crowed. But then he noticed that the sun was beginning to appear among the clouds. And he said:

"Dear sun, my good friend,
please dry out the water
that won't put out the fire
that won't burn the stick
that won't hit the dog
that won't bite the lamb
that won't eat the grass
that won't clean my beak
so that I can go to my own uncle's wedding."

And the sun answered:

"Of course I will. Every morning you greet me with your bright song, my friend. I will gladly dry out the water."

But then the water cried out:
"No, please don't dry me out. I will put out the fire."

And the fire cried out:
    "No, please don't put me out. I will burn the stick."

The stick, in turn, cried out:
    "No, please don't burn me. I will hit the dog."

But the dog cried out:
    "No, please don't hit me. I will bite the lamb."

So the lamb quickly cried out:
    "No, please don't bite me. I will eat the grass."

But the grass cried out very loudly:
"No, please don't eat me. I will clean the rooster's beak."

And before you know it the rooster's beak shone as
bright as the day.

So the rooster said good-bye to everyone with a happy
"Cock-a-doodle-doo!" and went on his way to his uncle's
wedding. And he walked with a brisk and springy walk, to
get there on time for the banquet.